TO ROSE AND CARMELO AND THEIR GREAT-GREAT-GRANDCHILDREN-TO-BE SM

FOR MY PARENTS, RALPH AND LESLEY RC

Scholastic Press
An imprint of Scholastic Australia Pty Limited
PO Box 579 Gosford NSW 2250
ABN 11 000 614 577
www.scholastic.com.au

Part of the Scholastic Group
Sydney · Auckland · New York · Toronto · London · Mexico City
New Delhi · Hong Kong · Buenos Aires · Puerto Rico

Published by Scholastic Australia in 2024.

NATIONAL LIBRARY OF AUSTRALIA
A catalogue record for this book is available from the National Library of Australia

ISBN: 978-1-76026-858-9 (hardback)
Rebel Challenger created these illustrations digitally.
Typeset in Bree Serif and Goodlife.

Printed in China by RR Donnelley.
Scholastic Australia's policy, in association with RR Donnelley, is to use papers that are renewable and made efficiently from wood grown in responsibly managed sources, so as to minimise its environmental footprint.

10 9 8 7 6 5 4 3 2 1 24 25 26 27 28 / 2

the IMPATIENT GLACIER

words by
Shaun Micallef

art by
Rebel Challenger

A Scholastic Press book from Scholastic Australia

A glacier up on a mountain
grew tired of the same boring view.
He wanted excitement; he wanted some fun.
He wanted to see something new.

He cancelled all the newspapers.
He put on his scarf and his hat.

He packed up his bag
and his lunchbox

and then left
after feeding the cat.

He started to move very slowly,
inching forward by only degrees.
It was getting him nowhere quite quickly
so he strapped on a new pair of skis.

Off he went with a push . . .

RIGHT INTO A BUSH!

He said, 'Hmm—that could have been better.'

He decided it best
to go by express
and post himself
there like a letter.

He wrapped himself
up in brown paper;

he tied himself tightly
with string;

he addressed himself
neatly with biro . . .

he looked a remarkable thing.

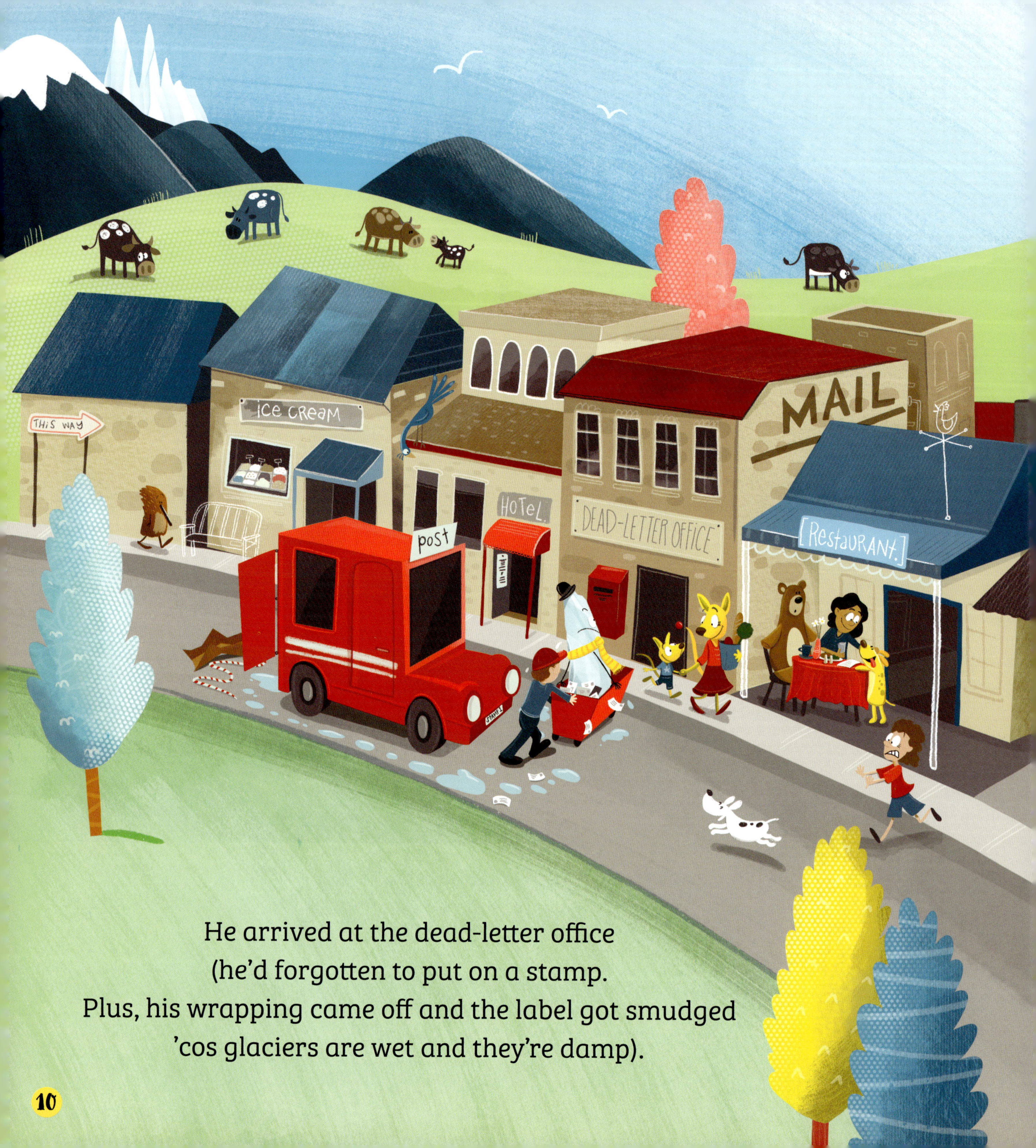

He arrived at the dead-letter office
(he'd forgotten to put on a stamp.
Plus, his wrapping came off and the label got smudged
'cos glaciers are wet and they're damp).

The impatient glacier was burning
with yearning and zeal and a zest.
But what was he after? To travel much faster!
He was not going to stop for a rest.

The glacier bought a train ticket,
shouting to all who would listen:

'COME ON,
LET'S GET GOING.
I DON'T HAVE
THE TIME!'

In the sun,
he had started
to glisten.

The train pulled out of the station
with a hiss and a big plume of steam,

while the glacier studied the map on his lap—
he was close to fulfilling his dream.

‘But couldn’t the train travel faster?’
the glacier said to himself.
To the furnace he raced with his bucket and spade,
ignoring the risk to his health.

He got to the town by the sea soon enough.
The beach was in reach!
He could feel it!

He waved down a family and asked for a lift,
climbing into the back of their Fiat.

He pointed and gestured and shouted directions,
'til he saw the sand of the seaside.

The Fiat pulled up. The glacier jumped out, saying, 'Thank you so much for the free ride!'

The impatient glacier was tiny.
He had melted a lot on the way.

He was now the shape and about the same size
of an ice cube you'd find in a tray.

He sat on the sand and saw the sun setting,
and knew his adventure was done.

It occurred to him then that it's **getting there**
that really is half of the fun.

But he'd totally missed the koala
in the tree on page seventeen,

or the frogs riding dogs
on page seven,

or the page before's
tooth-brushing bee.

All of the wonderful sights and sounds!
All of the beautiful things that abound!
Up in the sky or down on the ground,
there to enjoy . . . if he'd *just* looked around.

‘OH, I WISH I COULD DO IT ALL OVER AGAIN!’

said the ice cube from under his hat.

'I'd look out the window and stop now and then . . .
but I guess there's no chance of that.'

'We'll take you home,' the daughter declared.
'And we'll stop whenever you wish.
To look at that possum a few pages back;
the one playing cards with the fish.'

And after the father had packed up
the balls and the kite and the rug,
they all piled in and drove up the road . . .

and the little girl gave him a hug.